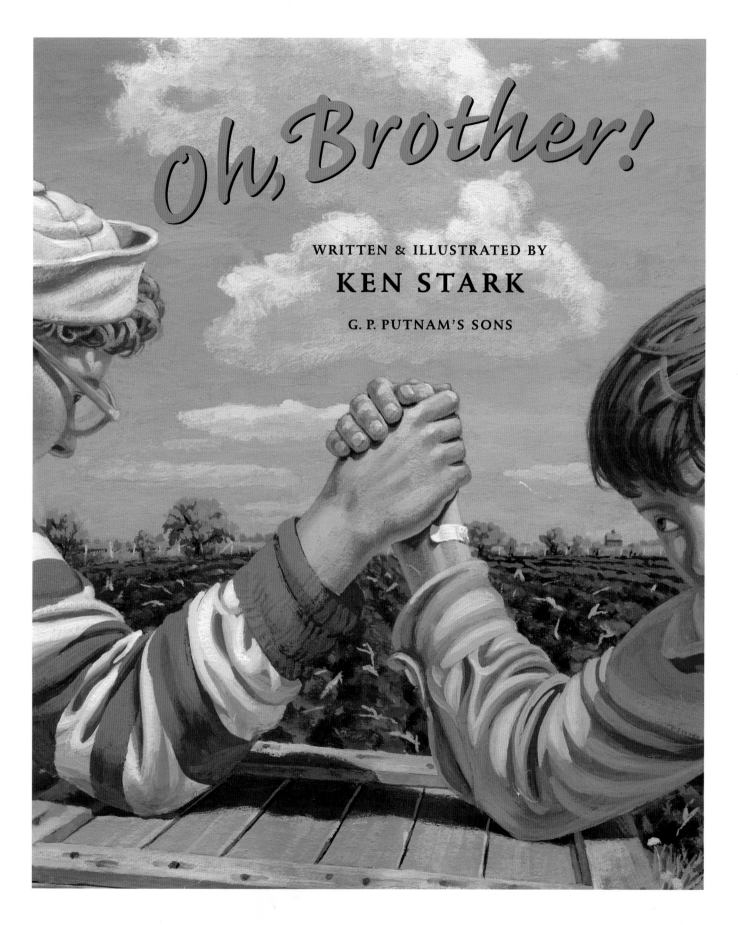

Oh, Brother!

WRITTEN & ILLUSTRATED BY

KEN STARK

G. P. PUTNAM'S SONS

My brother Phil and I grew up trying to outdo each other.

One day I saved his life. Well, not exactly. But I did run home to get Mom when he gashed his foot wading in a ditch. Then, a few weeks after that, Phil rescued me! You'll see how later.

We sure kept Mom hopping with Band-Aids and iodine. She raised us alone in this three-room house Grandpa Roat built near Kankakee, Illinois.

I was nine in 1952. Phil, a year older than me, was a lot taller and had big bones. I was always trying to beat him at something besides eating.

We boys liked living on Splear Road. We could see for miles, run forever, and yell our lungs out. None of us missed our old, gloomy house in town—even though it *did* have a bathroom.

To make ends meet, Mom took in ironing. Sometimes Phil and I could chip in a dollar each from hoeing the Splears' soybean field. Mom couldn't afford extra stuff like a phone, car, or TV.

That was okay. Just being in the country was enough. We could chase our imaginations anywhere.

Spring breezed through our door and smelled almost as good as Mom's Saturday-morning waffles. I plopped down at the rocking chair, my favorite place to eat. Our dog Echo and cats Butterball and Orphan Annie wouldn't get a single bite of *my* meal. They only got lucky when we had liver.

Our best friend and neighbor Tootie Splear came scouting for fun. Lickety-split, we climbed the apple tree to the chicken-house roof and flew off like Superman. Phil jumped the farthest.

"Wait until next time!" I said.

We were playing catch when the sky in the west turned black as the plowed fields.

"Man alive!" I said, gawking.

Mom cried, "Philip! Kenneth! Come in this instant!"

Phil got a head start. "Ken, don't just stand there!" he hollered.

I dashed off as the air crackled with lightning. Each flash was a stab of fear for Mom. But I wanted to watch from a tall tree, swaying way up in the middle of the storm.

Buzzy Meyers, Tootie's cousin, turned into the drive and pulled an old bicycle out of his truck.

"You boys want this?" he asked, his eyes twinkling.

Phil and I nodded in amazement. Our first bike!

Now we could go almost anywhere, even clear to the Shumans' farm. Nothing was better than swinging on ropes in their hayloft—*except* riding Pete, their pony.

We were strictly told not to touch the wringer washer. But I was curious. Before Phil could say "You'd better not!" I turned it on and touched the rollers. They grabbed my finger and started tearing it off! Phil hit the release button just in time.

"Oh, brother!" he said. "*Now* you've done it!"

I was embarrassed to tell kids at school how I got my wound. A sword-fight cut would have been better.

Phil figured we were big enough to mow the yard so Mom wouldn't have to pay someone. Pushing the rattly reel mower, though, wore us out so fast, we felt like pip-squeaks.

"Ooee," I grumped. "This'll take *forever*."

By supper time, we were pooped but proud. We did it!

A junky steering wheel Phil found by the road inspired us to build a Cloud Cruiser. It didn't have an engine, but we flew to Timbuktu anyway.

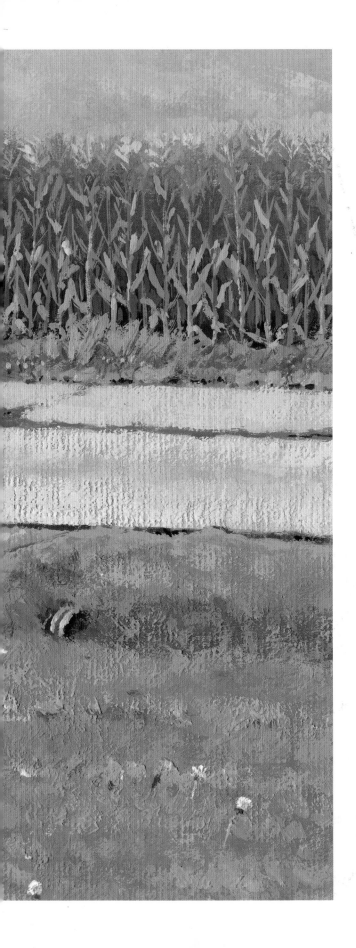

"The Ice Cream Man!" Tootie shouted, first to hear his bells. We all jumped up and ran.

He was dripping sweat from pedaling out so far. Phil got him a glass of water, and then we made our choices. I wanted a Popsicle because it was biggest and had two sticks. When the man reached into the mysterious icebox, we all took a peek. Winter swirled inside.

We got up early to see why in the world Echo was barking in the fog. The sight gave us goose bumps.

"Where did *he* come from?" Phil whispered, bug-eyed.

"Mom, he's in our yard. Can we keep him? *Please?*" I yearned.

We wanted to name him Flyer and ride bareback to school, but pretty soon Flyer's owners came to take him away. We rode the bus to school, as always.

Around Halloween, farmers left us kids a giant treat in the field right next to our house—a corncob pile!

At last I was King of the Mountain, until Phil took it back. Good thing Tootie and I liked tumbling to the bottom like stuntmen.

Shivering, we boys hauled in fuel oil after school and stole the cats' places by the heater. Right off Phil was glued to a car magazine, gazing at his first love . . . a Ford. Desperate for adventure, I grabbed our old bow and arrows.

"Careful, Robin Hood," Mom called, "you'll shoot your brother's eye out."

On Christmas Eve, we listened to every word of *A Christmas Carol* on the radio. Scrooge and Tiny Tim seemed to leap right out of London, into our living room!

The BIG snow came and made us as energetic as sled dogs. We tunneled through dazzling drifts, built a snowman whose belly we could barely lift, and had a major-league snowball fight. It was Tootie and me against Phil. He clobbered us anyway.

By then our sleeves were icy from wiping our noses. We were ready for cocoa, but not before a sneak attack . . . BULL'S-EYE!

Next to playing outside, drawing was our favorite thing. Sometimes we drew what we heard on radio dramas, like *Sergeant Preston of the Yukon*. This time, I made up action pictures of cowboys and spacemen. Phil sketched speeding, colliding cars that looked almost real. How I wished I could draw that well! He didn't even need an eraser. Mom gave all our drawings different scores, yet somehow our totals came out the same.

Mom had her own fun, laughing out loud at a book and writing a poem about Phil and me.

Meanwhile, winter wouldn't stay outside where it belonged. We could even see our breath in the bedroom. Mom warmed bricks on the heater, wrapped them in towels, and tucked them between the sheets.

That night, I poked my nose out of the covers. "Phil, guess what I'm going to do first when it's spring?"

"I give. What?" He yawned.

"Jump a MILE off the chicken-house roof!"

"Okay," said Phil. "I'll jump TWO miles!"

*In memory of my mom, Winifred Stark, who taught Phil and me
everything that matters. Her love softened the hard times
and kept us happy, despite her divorce and ailing health.*

*Special thanks to my wife Chris, brother Phil,
and friends Clayton and "Tootie" (Carolyn) Splear Pratt. —K.L.S.*